VIKING CONQUEST!

ReadZone Books Limited

First published in this edition 2017

© copyright in the text Stewart Ross 2017
© copyright in this edition ReadZone Books 2017

The right of the Author to be identified as the Author of this work
has been asserted by the Author in accordance with the Copyright,
Designs and Patents Act 1988.

Printed in Malta by Melita Press

British Library Cataloguing in Publication Data (CIP) is available
for this title.

ISBN 978 1 78322 624 5

Visit our website: www.readzonebooks.com

VIKING CONQUEST!

Stewart Ross

CONTENTS

TO THE READER

Viking Conquest! takes place early in the 11th century,
when Anglo-Saxons and Vikings (from Scandinavia)
were fighting to control England. The setting is real. So
are all the main characters: Edmund Ironside, Ethelred
the Unready, Canute, Lady Edith, and Lord Streona. The
events actually happened, too, and I've woven them
into this story to bring alive one of the most exciting
times in our eventful history.

Stewart Ross

THE STORY SO FAR ...

THE KINGDOM OF ENGLAND

After the death of Alfred the Great in 899, the Anglo-Saxon kings who succeeded him gradually won control over all England. By the time of King Edgar (959–975), England was one of the most settled, united and wealthy kingdoms in northern Europe. The Viking invaders, it seemed, had been defeated. But in 980 the attacks began again.

ETHELRED THE UNREADY

The king at this time was Ethelred, known as the 'Unready'. He got the nickname because people said he didn't listen to advice (or *rede* in the Anglo-Saxon language), not because he was unprepared.

The new wave of Scandinavian invaders came mostly from Denmark. They were led by Sweyn Forkbeard, King of Denmark and ruler of parts of Norway. Ethelred did not prove a very powerful leader. For example, he used the tactic of paying the invaders money – known as *Danegeld* – to go away. £10,000 was paid in 991, £16,000 in 994, £24,000 in 1002 and £48,000 in 1011. You can see what was happening: the more the English paid, the keener the Vikings were to come back for more!

KING SWEYN

In 1013, after much fighting, many English chose
Sweyn as their king. King Ethelred fled to Normandy
in northern France. This was where his second wife,
Emma, came from. But Ethelred's sons by his first wife –
Athelstan, Edmund and Eadwig – fought on against the
invader.

TWO KINGS

When Sweyn died in 1014, the Vikings – mostly Danes –
chose Sweyn's son, Canute, as their king. So when our
story starts, England had two Kings: (1) Ethelred, an
Englishman living in France; (2) Canute, a Dane, living
in England. Ethelred's warrior sons were determined to
keep the crown on an English head ...

TIME LINE

CE (Common Era)

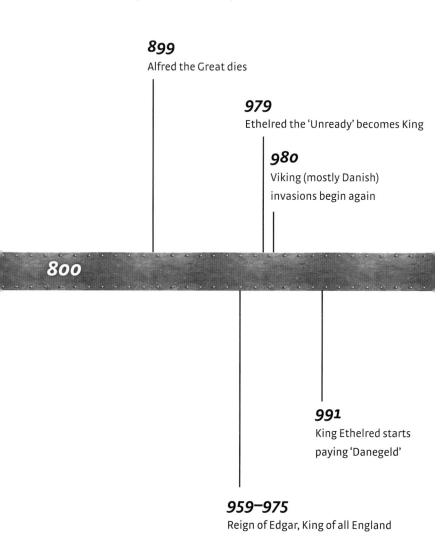

899
Alfred the Great dies

979
Ethelred the 'Unready' becomes King

980
Viking (mostly Danish)
invasions begin again

800

991
King Ethelred starts
paying 'Danegeld'

959–975
Reign of Edgar, King of all England

1016

King Ethelred dies; Edmund Ironside chosen
King of England
18 October: Battle of Assandun
King Edmund dies; Canute crowned King of England

1015

Canute leads massive invasion of England

1002

Ethelred's first wife dies; he marries
Emma of Normandy
Ethelred orders the massacre of all
Danes living in England

1020

1013

Sweyn declared King of England
Ethelred flees to Normandy

1014

Sweyn dies; Vikings choose his son,
Canute, as King of England
The English force Canute back to
Denmark; Ethelred returns

1003

Sweyn Forkbeard invades England

Chapter 1

FIGHT ON, DEAR BROTHER!

The moment Prince Edmund entered the darkened room, he knew why his brother had sent for him. There was no avoiding the smell of death.

Taking a deep breath, Edmund did his best to hide his feelings. 'You look better, Athelstan,' he said, peering down at the pale face on the bed beneath him.

Athelstan opened his eyes. 'Better?' he asked, his voice no more than a whisper. 'Yes, brother, I hope I will soon be much, much better.'

'I'm sure you will.'

'Edmund. I trust I will soon be with God in Heaven.' He closed his eyes again.

'But no...' began Edmund. He left the sentence unfinished. There was no point in pretending any longer. Athelstan was too clever – he knew the fever that had gripped him for the last week was gradually, hour by hour, carrying him away; and there was nothing he could do to stop it. Soon, probably before nightfall, Edmund's dear elder brother, the man with whom he had grown up, would be no more.

Edmund remembered their childhood, the happy hours they had played together in the grounds of their father's palace. Alas! Those bright days had been all too short. Their mother had died young, and war, like a fiery dragon, had stalked the land. Ever since their teens, the two boys had been warriors, fighting against the violent men from the north who were trying to seize England for themselves.

After a long silence, Athelstan spoke again. 'Will you promise me something, dear brother?'
Edmund went down on his knees beside the bed and took Athelstan's cold hand in his. 'Whatever you ask,' he replied, 'if it is in my power to grant, I swear by Almighty God to do so.'

'Then take my sword, brother, the great blade that was once carried by the mighty King Offa of Mercia.'

'But that sword –'

'You promised, Edmund. Take the sword, wear it with pride and use it to fight on, dear brother! Fight on until every Viking – be they from Denmark, Norway or Sweden – is driven from this land!'

They were the last words Athelstan spoke. After a fearful fit of coughing, he turned dreadfully pale and lost consciousness. An hour later, he was dead.

* * *

Athelstan was buried in the Great Church at Winchester. When the ceremony was over, Edmund rode off alone into the wooded hills above the town. He needed time to think.

After a couple of miles, he got off his horse and found a patch of open ground. *English ground*, he thought.

Not *Danish*!

He sighed and kicked angrily at the flints beneath his feet. *Why had his father fled across the Channel with his new French wife? He should be here with us, in England, leading his people against the invader.*

Athelstan and I did our best. But how could we persuade men to fight when their King himself wasn't here? And look what had happened! As soon as King Ethelred left, Canute, a teenage Danish prince, had started calling himself King of England. Worse still, a number of the English had accepted him.

That's part of the problem, Edmund realized. *I can't trust my own people. Not even my brother-in-law, Lord Streona of Mercia.*

Edmund lifted King Offa's great sword and whirled it round his head. 'Oh brother Athelstan!' he shouted to the heavens. 'Whatever happens, I will not let you down! I will obey your last wish: I – will – fight – on!'

Lowering the sword, Edmund rode back down the slope towards the town. He hadn't gone far when he noticed someone galloping towards him. He recognised the figure – it was his younger brother, Eadwig.

'Hello!' called Edmund as the two horses drew alongside each other. 'What brings you up here in such a hurry? Not more bad news, I hope?'

Eadwig grinned. 'No, brother. Quite the opposite.'

'Go on …'

'Our father the King has come back from France. He's promised to lead us against Canute straight away.'

Chapter 2

HE WILL BE BACK

Edmund knelt before his father. 'Great King and Father,' he began, 'We are so pleased you have returned to take command of the army.'

King Ethelred sniffed. 'Yes, yes, I know all that. As you've heard, I've promised to do what my people want.'

He turned to his new wife, Emma of Normandy. 'I'll be a better ruler now, won't I, my dearest?'

'Of course, my lord,' she smiled.

Edmund watched her carefully. *She smiled with her lips*, he thought, *but not with her eyes. She'd marry anyone just to be Queen!*

'And we'll tackle this Canute at once?' Edmund asked, rising to his feet.

The King looked confused. 'You mean now? I was thinking we'd wait until the weather was bit warmer and –'

'Father!' interrupted Edmund. He felt his face reddening as he tried to control his anger. 'The longer we wait, the stronger Canute will be. We must strike hard – and strike now!'

'Oh dear! No wonder they call you "Ironside!" Always keen on fighting, fighting, fighting! I've found that you only have to pay these Danes money – and they go away. No need for fighting at all.'

Edmund clenched his fists in annoyance. 'And when you pay them this Danegeld, Father, what do they do? They come back for more. And more. No, there is only one way to get rid of them forever, and that is with the sword!'

'Very well, very well,' tutted the King. 'Go and do whatever's necessary, Edmund Ironside.'

* * *

Edmund's reputation as a warrior went before him. When horsemen left London and rode through the countryside asking men to join a new royal army – led by Prince Ironside – they came in their thousands. By early April, the soldiers were ready to march north.

Meanwhile, Edmund's scouts reported that Canute was in Lindsey, south of the River Humber. He was trying to put together an army of his own. The locals had promised him men and horses – but Edmund's swift action had taken them by surprise.

Spring came early that year. As the King marched north across the Chiltern Hills and over the broad streams of the Rivers Ouse and Trent, the orchards were bright with blossom. *Flowers are a good sign*, thought Edmund. *Even nature is welcoming us.*

He was right. When the English army reached Lindsey, Canute had gone. Rather than risk battle, he had taken to his ships and sailed back to Denmark. King Ethelred was delighted.

'Ah! Just as I like it,' he chortled as he sat at dinner with his family and other English noblemen. 'Victory without fight. Always the best way. That's why I decided to move quickly, before this Canute fellow had time to get ready.'

Edmund looked across at Eadwig and raised an eyebrow. They both knew the speed of attack had been Ironside's idea, not the King's.

'And now,' continued Ethelred with a smile, 'We must execute all those men of Lindsey who were planning to fight for Canute.'

'Execute?' interrupted Edmund. 'I don't think that would be wise, Father. The people of Lindsey hate Canute for running away. They are our allies now.'

The King looked at his son and shook his head. 'Is Ironside going soft?' he sneered. 'Is he now Butterside? No mercy, Edmund. The men who were prepared to fight against us must die. I am King and I order it!'

Later that night, after the King had retired, Edmund and Eadwig met to discuss their father's decision.

'I don't like it,' said the younger brother. 'Many good soldiers will lose their lives, and many fine women will be left bitter widows. Our father is not a great one for making friends, is he?'

Edmund nodded. 'No. You know what they call him behind his back, don't you?'

'Yes. "King No-advice" – because he always thinks he knows best and won't listen to anyone else.'

'Wish he'd listened to us, Eadwig. I really do. One day

soon we're going to need every able-bodied Englishman we can find.'

'Why?'

'Because Canute will be back. Oh yes, he'll be back all right.'

Chapter 3

MURDER AND MARRIAGE

As spring gave way to summer, relations between
Edmund and his father grew worse. The prince wanted
to strengthen the navy and build up the army ready for
another Viking attack. But Ethelred would hear none of
it. He was still obsessed with taking revenge on those
who had helped the Danes.

In mid-June, things came to a head at a council
meeting in Oxford.

Prince Edmund went to meet his father as soon as
he arrived. He found him alone with Lord Streona, the
prince's brother-in-law. The two men moved quickly
apart when Edmund entered.

'Oh! I hope I haven't disturbed a private meeting,'
he said.

Streona's shifty grey eyes narrowed. 'Not at all, dear
Edmund. Your father and I have said all we need to. Isn't
that right, Sire?'

The King nodded. 'Indeed, we have finished. All is
arranged.'

Ah! thought Edmund. *So they have been up to
something. I wonder what it is?*

He found out when the council met again the very
next day.

When everyone was in their place, the King stood up

and began his speech. How glad he and his wife were to be back in England, he said. Now he had driven off the Danes, all England was safe once more.

Oh yes? queried Edmund. His thoughts were interrupted by the King.

'And to make us doubly safe, I had the traitors of Lindsey executed. But their leaders, Lords Sigeferth and Morcar, were spared. That was a mistake. I invited them here to Oxford to receive their punishment.'

That's not what I heard, thought Edmund, glancing at Eadwig. *Sigeferth and Morcar were told they were coming here to be pardoned, not punished.*

Edmund's thoughts were once more interrupted by the King.

'To save us the trouble, Lord Streona of Mercia has already carried out their punishment. He executed both the traitors last night.'

A gasp of surprise ran through the hall. 'I have seized their lands,' the King continued, 'and imprisoned Lady Edith, Sigeferth's wife, in Malmsbury Abbey.'

Edmund could take no more. Jumping to his feet, he cried, 'My lord, you may be the King and you may be my father, but I cannot accept this behaviour. Those men were not executed. They were murdered – yes, murdered! That is not the way of English justice!'

Leaving his words ringing in the rafters, Edmund stormed from the hall.

He knew exactly what he had to do. Taking a small band of trusted servants, he rode hard to Malmsbury.

He arrived early the next day, went straight to the Abbey gatehouse, and demanded to be let in. When the guards saw who it was, they opened up immediately.

Edmund found Edith sitting alone in a small cell. They had often met before and at one time it was even rumoured they might marry. Although nothing came of it, they remained good friends.

'Edmund!' she cried as he came in. 'What on earth ...?'

'No time to explain,' he said, taking her hand and guiding her towards the door. 'You're free – so come with me. I'll tell you everything later. But now we must get as far away as possible.'

* * *

The couple fled to the Danelaw, the area of eastern England that had once been in Viking hands. Edith was popular there. So was Edmund – the locals had heard how he had opposed his father's cruel executions.

Edith had never been very fond of her husband and, as the weeks passed, she came to terms with his violent end. His place in her heart was taken by Edmund.

'You know, Edith,' he said as they were walking together one day, 'I always regretted that we didn't get married before, when we were such good friends.'

'But we're still very good friends, Edmund dear.'

He paused and turned towards her. 'Then, Edith, will you ...?'

'Of course I will!'

The couple were married a week later. The day was one of the happiest Edmund could remember – until, in the middle of the wedding feast, a mud-splattered messenger staggered into the hall.

'My lord!' he cried. 'Canute is back. He has landed in England with an army of 10,000 Viking warriors!'

Chapter 4

ABANDONED!

The next morning Edmund and Lady Edith called a council of war. Prince Eadwig was there, together with half-a-dozen of the most powerful lords of the Danelaw and the north of England.

They could certainly defeat Canute, they agreed, but only if all the English acted together. Trying to avoid Edmund, the Viking army had landed in Wessex, in the south. To meet it, suggested Edmund, his forces should join with those of London and Mercia.

'Mercia?' interrupted Edith. 'Mercia is under the control of Streona, the man who murdered my husband. Do you really think we can trust someone like that?'

Edmund looked embarrassed. 'I know, Edith. But what else can we do? Relations with my father are bad enough. If we fall out openly with Streona as well, Canute will be laughing. He'll be able to pick us off one by one. We must at least try to act together.'

'All right,' said Edith. 'But we must be very, very careful.'

That afternoon, Edmund sent riders with letters for the King in London and for Streona in Gloucester. The plan was to hold London as a base while the King led an English army against Canute's Vikings. If they all trusted each other, Edmund wrote, and if they were led by the King, victory would be theirs.

And I will have kept my promise to my dying brother, he thought.

As they stood watching the messengers ride away, Edith asked, 'Surely we can manage without your father? Everyone knows what a poor leader he is.'

'Yes, they do,' replied Edmund. 'But he's still the King, and his crown is the symbol of England. We may not respect him, Edith, but I'm afraid we need him.'

Edmund was right. When he told them that the King would lead the fight against the invader, warriors flocked to join Ironside's army. By the end of the summer he had many thousands under his command.

But there was still no reply from London or Gloucester.

The first news finally came one drizzly afternoon in early September. Edmund's favourite commander, Ubba Galwin, came squelching through the rain with a confused look on his face.

'Well, Ubba, what is it?'

'News from your brother-in-law, my lord. Lord Streona and his army will meet us at Oxford on the first day of October. With the King at our head, he will then march with us against the enemy.'

'But that's good news, eh? Why the puzzled look?'

Ubba shook his shaggy head like a dog, sending a shower of raindrops in all directions. 'It's what he says about the King, my lord. What happens if your father doesn't show up?'

'He will, Ubba,' said Edmund. 'He will.' His words sounded positive, but in his heart he was a lot less certain.

As agreed, the forces of Streona and Edmund marched to Oxford and set up camp a few hundred paces apart. The two commanders met between the camps and shook hands. Streona grinned slyly and asked whether Edmund had forgiven him for 'executing' the traitors, Sigeferth and Morcar.

'All that is in the past,' muttered Edmund. 'We have something more important to focus on.'

Streona smiled. 'Ah yes,' he drawled. 'Defeating the Vikings. I do hope your father will get here soon.'

'He'll be here before long,' replied Edmund. 'Wait and see.'

But the King did not come. Instead, he sent a message saying he was ill, and Edmund and Streona should fight on without him. Edmund's heart sank.

'I think it might be best to call off the campaign,' advised Edith when he told her. 'We can't fight beside someone we can't trust.'

Edmund agreed. As it turned out, the decision was made for him. When he woke the next morning and looked towards the Mercian camp, there was not a soul to be seen. During the night, Streona and his men had packed up their belongings and left.

Three days later, Edmund and Edith received the news they feared most. Streona had joined forces with Canute.

Chapter 5

KING EDMUND

As soon as he heard Streona was fighting alongside Canute, Edmund called a meeting with Edith, Eadwig and Ubba.

'Well?' he asked. 'Press on or return to our lands in the Danelaw?'

'One great victory will do it,' rumbled Ubba. 'So I vote we attack. If we fail … well, we die only once – and what finer way to go than fighting for our country?'

'But I'm not sure our men will fight for Wessex,' said Eadwig. 'They'll fight to protect their own lands, sure. But now we're here, far from home, they'll fight for just one thing.'

'What's that?' asked Ubba.

'The crown worn by the King of England.'

Edith nodded. 'And as the King is not with us, our men may not fight.'

'I have heard mutterings already,' said Edmund. 'The soldiers keep asking where my father is. When I say he's sick, they shrug and turn away.'

'Then I think that answers our question,' said Edith. 'We have no choice but to return to the Danelaw.'

No one disagreed.

* * *

The retreat back to Edmund and Edith's homelands marked the beginning of a grim winter. Without the King's support, they found it difficult to hold their army together. The news from London was always the same: King Ethelred was sick. He would join his sons as soon as he was well again.

By Christmas the outlook was darker still. Canute and Streona had crossed the River Thames and were striking north. Further urgent messages were sent to London, and still the King did not come. During January and February, more and more land fell into Viking hands.

Edmund was confident he could stop the rot if he could bring Canute to battle. But whenever he advanced, the crafty Dane slipped away without fighting.

In March Edmund Ironside had had enough. 'If my father the King won't come to me,' he said angrily to Edith, 'We'll have to go to him'.

'To London?'

'Yes, my love. We leave tomorrow.'

Secure behind massive walls built by the Romans many centuries earlier, London had resisted every Viking attack. However, inside the royal palace, all was far from well.

The moment Edmund saw his father, he was reminded of his dying brother, Athelstan. The same pale face and empty, red-rimmed eyes. The same smell in the air, too – the sickly, sad smell of death.

Father and son both knew the truth. They forgave

past quarrels, and the King asked Edith to forgive him for imprisoning her in Malmsbury Abbey after the murder of her first husband.

'I have forgotten it already,' she smiled. 'After all, if I had not been locked up, Edmund would never have come to rescue me ...'

King Ethelred died two weeks after Easter. The death of a king is always a sorrowful occasion, but this was perhaps less sorrowful than most. Edmund and Edith, now King and Queen of England, knew this as well as anyone.

'He did his best,' Edith observed kindly as they walked away from Ethelred's grave in the church of St Paul.

'Possibly. But it wasn't very good, was it?'

Edith took his hand in hers. 'Not like the new King, eh? I'm sure that under King Edmund, all will be well again!'

The people agreed with her. The Londoners cheered whenever he appeared in the streets. Some days later, Edmund ventured into nearby Essex. Here, too, he was warmly welcomed.

'Long live King Edmund!' they shouted. 'Death to the Vikings!'

When he asked whether the menfolk would be willing to join his army and fight against Canute, they replied that they'd do anything for him. With King Edmund Ironside at their head, they declared, victory was certain.

Chapter 6

THE RETURN OF STREONA

What a glorious summer it was! It began with Edmund's victorious march into Wessex. The leaders of that ancient kingdom, he heard, had met at Southampton and accepted Canute as their King.

'Never!' Ironside cried when he was told the news. 'The kingdom of Alfred the Great surrendering to the Vikings? Shame on them!'

Gathering his army, he crossed the Thames and smashed every force Canute sent against him. By July, as his men were beginning to think of bringing in the harvest, all Wessex was once more loyal to Edmund, King of England. The name 'Ironside' was on everyone's lips, and songs were sung in his honour.

But Canute, though still a young man, was clever and careful. He had avoided meeting Edmund in battle personally. Instead, he sneaked round behind him and attacked London. Once again, Edmund moved with great speed. This time he was helped by Ubba.

Ironside proposed advancing along the Thames and attacking the Vikings head on.

'But I believe I have a better plan, my lord,' said the old soldier. 'I was born and brought up in London and I know the area very well. You want to move in from the west. Canute will be expecting that. I suggest we go round to the north.'

'The north? Why?'

'Because there are many secret paths through the woods near the village of Tottenham. If you allow me to lead you, I can show you how to take the enemy completely by surprise.'

And so it was. Charging out of the woods at dawn, the English hurled the Vikings back to their ships, and they escaped down the river. Two days later, Edmund launched another attack, this time at Brentford. Once more the Vikings were defeated – and once more Canute himself escaped unharmed.

On and on the fighting went, though the hot days of August and into the autumn. Wherever Canute went, Ironside followed him.

'It's only a matter of time,' he told his brother Eadwig after they had chased the Vikings out of Kent and on to the Isle of Sheppey. 'They're running out of horses, their men are exhausted, and even the weather is turning against them. It won't be long now before Canute comes begging for mercy.'

'And will you show him any?'

'Of course. As long as he agrees to leave my kingdom and never return.'

'But take care, brother. He's a slippery customer. A bit like Streona, your brother-in-law. Not to be trusted.'

Edmund laughed. 'Streona? He's learned his lesson by now. I bet every day he regrets going over to Canute.' The King fingered the great sword at his side. 'In fact,

I wouldn't be surprised if he came crawling back to us.'

'If he did, would you take him back, Edmund?'

'I'm not sure. It'd depend how genuinely sorry he was. He'd certainly have to answer a few questions if he did show up.'

And he did show up. Surrounded by his bodyguard, Streona entered the English camp one drizzly October afternoon. On seeing Edmund, he fell to his knees on the muddy ground.

'Sire,' he cried, 'Forgive me!'

Edmund strode up and stood above him. 'Forgive you, traitor? Why should I?'

Streona raised his shifty grey eyes. 'Because I am sorry – with all my heart – for what I did.'

'Oh yes?'

'And because I have information, my lord, that will enable you to defeat Canute once and for all.'

Chapter 7

ONE LAST BATTLE

At that moment, Queen Edith came to stand beside her husband. 'I don't believe it!' she said quietly, laying a hand on Edmund's arm and staring down at the visitor. Then, more loudly, 'I am surprised, Lord Streona of Mercia, that you dare even come near the King. I had hoped we would never set eyes on you again.'

The Queen's words seemed to confuse the grey-eyed nobleman, and it was a few seconds before he replied. 'Er, my Lady, I did not expect ...'

'Yes? What did you not expect?'

Streona looked across at Edmund. 'I did not expect to find a lady in a camp of war.'

'The Queen may not carry a sword,' said Edmund, 'But she is my most intelligent and wisest advisor'.

'Then she will appreciate my news,' replied Streona with an attempt at a smile.

'I doubt it,' said Edith. 'You murdered my first husband, Sigeferth, because he sided with Canute. You have done the same – so I see no reason why you too should not die. Except that we will give you a fair trial, and not just kill you like a dog.'

'How kind!' sneered Streona. 'But hear me first. Please,' he added, speaking the last word as if he were praying.

Edmund glanced across at Edith, who shrugged. 'All right,' he said. 'What do you have to say?'

'May I stand up, Sire?'

'No!' snapped Edith before her husband could reply. 'The dirt suits you.'

Streona nodded calmly. 'Very well. What I have to say is this. First, I have 2,000 men at my command. All experienced and skilful warriors. If they join your army, you will have enough men to crush the Vikings.'

'Perhaps,' said Edmund. 'But I believe we can defeat them as we are.'

'Maybe. But what I have to tell you will make that victory more certain.'

Streona looked around and lowered his voice to little more than a whisper. 'Canute needs supplies and horses. He intends to move to Essex and ravage the countryside. It is rich land and he will find what he wants there. But he will also find what he does not want.'

'Meaning?'

'You, Sire. If you cross London Bridge quickly and advance into Essex, you will surprise him. The Vikings will be trapped and Canute will be at your mercy. Our combined forces will destroy him. Utterly.'

Once more the words of the dying Athelstan ran through Edmund's mind: 'Fight on until every Viking is driven from this land!'

And here was an opportunity to fulfil his brother's last wish. But it meant trusting a traitor ....

'The Queen and I will discuss the matter in private,' said Edmund. 'Meanwhile, you remain here.'

The King and Queen walked some distance away. 'Well?'

'I think you know what I think, Edmund,' said Edith. 'The man is not to be trusted.'

'He has a record of looking out for himself, certainly. Whatever the situation, he likes to be on the winning side. Perhaps it's a good sign that he wishes to rejoin us?'

'Perhaps. But that won't make me like him. Or trust him.'

Edmund thought for a moment. 'All right. This is what we will do. We'll take up Streona's offer, but only on one condition. He must take Ubba and half-a-dozen of our best men into his army. They will serve as his bodyguard and watch his every move. If he does anything suspicious, they'll report back to us immediately. Agreed?'

'It might work.'

'Good. Then we'll give it a go. All we need is one last battle ….'

Chapter 8

VIKING CONQUEST!

In the fading light of an October evening, Edmund and Eadwig surveyed the scene. Before them stood a low, wooded hill known locally as Assandun. Canute's Viking army was spread along the lower slopes and among the trees on the summit.

'It's a strong position,' said Eadwig eventually. 'That Canute, he may be young, but he knows how to manage an army.'

Edmund grunted. 'Mmm. But he's beatable, brother. It'll cost us a few lives, but victory will be ours in the end.'

'So what do we do?'

Edmund explained his plan. He and most of the English army would attack straight up the hill. They would be at a huge disadvantage. But their numbers were greater than Canute's, and he would need most of his men to beat off the assault. That would leave the other side of the hill poorly defended ....

'Ah!' cried Eadwig. 'So while we draw most of the enemy to this side, Streona sneaks round to the other side and attacks the Vikings in the rear?'

'Precisely!'

'And you think Streona will do it?'

Edmund nodded. 'He's done everything right so far, brother. Ubba says his behaviour's been perfect. As I said before, he likes being on the winning side, so I think we can trust him to stay loyal.

'Go and fetch him here, please, and we'll explain our idea to him.'

When Streona heard the battle plan, he smiled in agreement. 'Excellent, Sire. I will do just as you command. My men will follow me, and we will triumph. The curse of the men from the north will finally be ended.'

After checking the details of the attack one last time, Edmund shook Streona by the hand and bid him goodnight.

'Tomorrow,' the Mercian lord called as he disappeared into the night, 'You will see what I am made of, Sire'.
I certainly will, thought Edmund. *I certainly will.*

* * *

The day dawned cold and clear. Canute's army had not moved during the night, and when it was light enough Edmund Ironside lined up his men facing the hill. He took a position in the front of the line with Eadwig at his side. A messenger brought news that, on the other side of the hill, Streona and his men were poised for their surprise attack. All was ready.

A trumpet blared, and the English moved forward up the lower slopes. As they advanced, Edmund noticed – just as he had planned – that Canute had brought his whole army to face them.

And the other side of the hill will be undefended, said Edmund to himself. *Perfect! As Streona advances, we'll have Canute caught like a rat in a trap!*

The two armies met with a fearful crash. Swords sliced, spears pierced, axes smashed helmets and heads. Yells and screams cut the air, and the green grass of the hillside ran red with blood.

In the midst of the battle, Edmund Ironside fought like a lion. Beneath the great sword his brother had given him, Vikings fell on every side. And all the while he kept an eye on the top of the hill, waiting for Streona and his men to reach the summit and close the trap.

But Streona did not come. When Edmund was beginning to wonder what had happened, out of the corner of his eye he saw a familiar figure staggering towards him. It was Ubba!

'My lord!' he panted. 'We are betrayed! Streona has killed all his bodyguard except me and is leading his men away from the battlefield. We fight alone!'

Edmund let out a terrible groan. The English would never be able to fight their way to the top of the hill. Defeat, like a giant hawk, hovered above them. In a moment, it would swoop down and seize them in its terrible, cruel claws.

'O brother Athelstan!' cried Edmund in a voice cracking with sorrow and shame. 'Forgive me! I promised to drive out the Vikings. I have failed. My reign has brought nothing but cruel Viking conquest!'

THE HISTORY FILE

WHAT HAPPENED NEXT?

Edmund Ironside

Owing to Streona's treachery, King Edmund Ironside lost the Battle of Assandun. It was a bitter defeat from which he never recovered. Wounded, he fought on before coming to a settlement with Canute. Edmund would rule Wessex, south of the River Thames, and Canute would rule Mercia, the Danelaw and the lands north of the river. They agreed that when one of them died, the other would become King of the whole kingdom.

Edmund died just a few weeks later, on 30 November 1016. His death remains a mystery. Some say he died of his wounds, others that he was murdered by Canute. Whichever is true, it made no difference: all England was now ruled by a Viking (Danish) King.

Edmund and Edith had two sons, Edward the Exile and Edmund Atheling. When Canute became King, he sent the two boys to Sweden where he wanted them killed. They escaped, however, and lived exciting lives in different parts of Europe. Their mother, Edith, may have gone with them, but there is no mention of her after Edmund Ironside's death.

And Streona? Canute trusted him even less than Edmund had done, and had him killed at Christmas, 1017.

Canute

Canute – also spelled Cnut – ruled England until 1035. His reign was successful, and he is sometimes known as Canute 'the Great' because he was also King of Denmark, Norway and part of Sweden. This made him one of the most powerful figures in all Europe.

Most people remember King Canute because of the story that he got his feet wet when he ordered the tide not to come in. Actually, this story is usually told wrongly. The men and women of the King's court flattered him by saying he was so powerful that even the waves would obey him. Canute said that was nonsense. To prove it, he stood on the shore and told the tide not to come in. It did, of course – and so the King showed his courtiers how foolish they were.

HOW DO WE KNOW?

Historians learn about the life and times of Edmund Ironside and Canute in two ways. One is by reading manuscripts written at, or near, the time; the other is by studying objects remaining from that period of history.

The most famous document is the *Anglo-Saxon Chronicle*. This is a record of important events. It was kept by monks from several monasteries, such as Abingdon, Worcester and Peterborough. These monks wrote down what they had heard and what they thought was important. Not surprisingly, they did not all record the same things.

We can also read *The Chronicle of Henry of Huntingdon*, written just over 100 years after Edmund's death. The book is full of interesting details and little stories, although there's no way of telling whether or not they are true. Other pieces of written information include such things as laws and poems – poets at the court of King Canute sang his praises loud and clear!

The job of the historian is to put together these different accounts, like a jigsaw, to produce a single story. Even so, there are many pieces missing. For instance, we don't even know where Assandun was.

There are few physical remains from the early 11th century. No English buildings survive, for example. But digging in the ground, archaeologists uncover all kinds of interesting artefacts. These are objects that have not rotted away, such as bricks, stones, bones, coins, jewellery and weapons. We use these to help us paint a more accurate picture of those distant but fascinating times.

NEW WORDS

Abbey
Church belonging to a monastery.

Archaeology
Finding out about the past by examining ancient buildings and artefacts.

Artefact
Anything made by a human being.

Campaign
Army's actions over a period of time, often involving one or more battles.

Cell
Small room in a monastery or prison.

Chronicle
Historical story.

Council
Important meeting of several people.

Danegeld
Money paid to Danish invaders to leave England.

Danelaw
Area of eastern England where Danes and other Scandinavians settled.

Execute
Punish someone by killing them.

Invade
Attack another land.

Lindsey
Part of modern-day Lincolnshire.

Manuscript
Handwritten document.

Mercia
Middle kingdom of Anglo-Saxon England.

Monastery
Buildings with a church or chapel where monks live.

Normandy
Area of northern France settled by the Vikings (North Men).

Rafters
Open wooden beams holding up a roof.

Ravage
To attack fiercely.

Scandinavia
Denmark, Norway, Sweden, and Finland.

Succeed
To take the crown after a king or queen has died.

Traitor
Someone who betrays their country or their people.

Viking
Name given to the people from Scandinavia who attacked England during the 8th, 9th, 10th and 11th centuries.

Wessex
Kingdom of the Saxons in southwest England.

Normandy
Area of northern France settled by the Vikings (North Men).

TIMELINERS
BRING HISTORY ALIVE!

978-1-78322-549-1

978-1-78322-559-0

978-1-78322-560-6

978-1-78322-547-7

978-1-78322-548-4

978-1-78322-567-5

978-1-78322-565-1

978-1-78322-566-8

978-1-78322-561-3

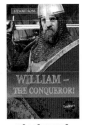

978-1-78322-537-8

978-1-78322-568-2

978-1-78322-592-7

This series by Stewart Ross really sends the reader
back into history! Each exciting book brings the past alive
by linking key events to a fast-moving narrative.